WITHDRAWN

For my baby granddaughter, Angelina
J. C.

For Fred
C. F.

First U.S. edition 2016

Library of Congress Catalog Card Number 2015941681

ISBN 978-0-7636-8662-8

15 16 17 18 19 20 FGF 10 9 8 7 6 5 4 3 2 1

Printed in Shenzhen, Guangdong, China

This book was typeset in Bell MT.

The illustrations were done in watercolor and ink.

Nosy Crow

an imprint of

Candlewick Press

99 Dover Street

Somerville, Massachusetts 02144

www.nosycrow.com

www.candlewick.com

WHO WOKE THE BABY?

Jane Clarke

illustrated by Charles Fuge

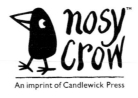

nosy crow™

An imprint of Candlewick Press

This is the **baby**

who woke in the morn,

smelly and **yelly**

and all forlorn.

This is the **hippo** whose yawn like a horn

woke the baby up in the morn,

smelly and **yelly** and all forlorn.

This is the **zebra** who made a **fuss**
that woke up Hippopotamus,
who yawned a yawn as loud as a **horn,**
that woke the baby up in the morn,
smelly and **yelly** and all forlorn.

This is the **lion** woken from snoring

who woke up Zebra with his **roaring.**

No wonder Zebra made a **fuss**

that woke up Hippopotamus,

who yawned a yawn as loud as a **horn,**

that woke the baby up in the morn,

smelly and **yelly** and all forlorn.

This is the **crocodile**, snippety-snap,
who woke up Lion from his nap.
Lion stopped his dreamy **snoring**
and woke up Zebra with his **roaring**.

No wonder Zebra made a **fuss**

that woke up Hippopotamus,

who yawned a yawn as loud as a **horn,**

that woke the baby up in the morn,

smelly and **yelly** and all forlorn.

This is the **frog** who croaked a **croak**

so **loud** that Crocodile awoke

and thrashed about, **snippety-snap,**

and woke up Lion from his nap.

Lion stopped his dreamy **snoring**

and woke up Zebra with his **roaring.**

No wonder Zebra made a **fuss**

that woke up Hippopotamus,

who yawned a yawn as loud as a **horn,**

that woke the baby up in the morn,

smelly and **yelly** and all forlorn.

This is the **bee,** all **striped** and **fuzzy,**
who woke up Frog by being so **buzzy.**
Busy Bee's **buzzing** made Frog **croak**
so **loud** that Crocodile awoke
and thrashed about, **snippety-snap,**
and woke up Lion from his nap.

Lion stopped his dreamy **snoring**

and woke up Zebra with his **roaring.**

No wonder Zebra made a **fuss**

that woke up Hippopotamus,

who yawned a yawn as loud as a **horn,**

that woke the baby up in the morn.

Poor little
baby,
all forlorn.

This is the
beautiful
butterfly . . .

who **fluttered**

through the dawning sky
and touched down gently, as you see,
on a flower next to Bee.

Busy Bee **buzzed** and made Frog **croak**
so **loud** that Crocodile awoke . . .

and thrashed about, **snippety-snap,**

and woke up Lion from his nap.

Lion stopped his dreamy **snoring**

and woke up Zebra with his **roaring.**

No wonder Zebra made a **fuss**

that woke up Hippopotamus,

who yawned a yawn as loud as a **horn,**

that woke the baby up in the morn.

This is the **baby**
who woke in the morn,
wriggly and **giggly**,
no longer forlorn.

This is the baby,
full of **delight**,
watching the butterfly
dance in the light.

This is the baby,

all **smiling** and **clappy**.

A **new** day has dawned

and **everyone's** happy.